About the Author

Dennis Piervicenti is a seventy-seven-year-old man retired from a half-century of various social service positions both high and low and a husband and father with more questions than answers, waiting for wisdom to suddenly appear.

Thoughts Fully Baked

Dennis Piervicenti

Thoughts Fully Baked

Olympia Publishers
London

www.olympiapublishers.com
OLYMPIA PAPERBACK EDITION

Copyright © Dennis Piervicenti 2024

The right of Dennis Piervicenti to be identified as author of
this work has been asserted in accordance with sections 77 and 78 of
the Copyright, Designs and Patents Act 1988.

All Rights Reserved

No reproduction, copy or transmission of this publication
may be made without written permission.
No paragraph of this publication may be reproduced,
copied or transmitted save with the written permission of the publisher,
or in accordance with the provisions
of the Copyright Act 1956 (as amended).

Any person who commits any unauthorized act in relation to
this publication may be liable to criminal
prosecution and civil claims for damage.

A CIP catalogue record for this title is
available from the British Library.

ISBN: 978-1-80439-820-3

This is a work of fiction.
Names, characters, places and incidents originate from the writer's
imagination. Any resemblance to actual persons, living or dead, is
purely coincidental.

First Published in 2024

Olympia Publishers
Tallis House
2 Tallis Street
London
EC4Y 0AB

Printed in Great Britain

Dedication

I dedicate this book to my wife Susan and daughter Jessica who for some reason think I'm a good person.

Acknowledgments

I want to thank my wife Susan for her feedback and carefully couched constructive criticism during the writing of this book.

Introduction

The stories contained here were the product of a pandemic inspired hibernation.

They slipped out of the narrow space between wisdom and senility and therefore contain no useful lessons. And most of the ideas posited contain only an accidental resemblance to fact.

They do, however, represent over seventy years of navel gazing and an attempt to impress upon my long-deceased homemaker mother and Teamster truck driver father that there was a point in majoring in philosophy in the sixties rather than their preference – physical education.

1
God Takes a Meeting

GABRIEL: *These briefing sessions are getting longer and longer. Why do we even have to have them if He... you know... if He like knows everything – with all due respect.*

ST. PETER: *I know, I know. But at His age, His omniscience is not what it used to be. Don't get me wrong – not much gets by Him – it just takes him longer to get to all of it. He's up to snuff right through Watergate but not much since. No wonder given all that's been on His plate, like nuclear proliferation, black holes and the Jets. While He has always had to shoulder the blame for any havoc wreaked by lousy weather, at least He is quite heartened of late by all the environmentalists placing the responsibility on man for stuff about oceans, hurricanes, fires, and temperatures being hotter than you know what.*

But He knows nothing about the whole COVID-19 pandemic thing and therefore today's meeting is to flesh out some of the details for Him.

Has everyone RSVP'd for today?

GABRIEL: *Just about. Einstein, FDR, Heidegger, Plath, Chisolm, Freud, Sartre, and Hitchens will all be here. Marx had a conflict and sends his apologies. And...*

ST. PETER: *Karl or Groucho?*

GABRIEL: *Karl. Was I supposed to invite Groucho?*

ST. PETER: *No, no, although it would have been nice. He's a big fan of* A Day at the Races.

GABRIEL: *We also have Toklas, Shakespeare, and Truman.*

ST. PETER: *Harry or Capote?*

GABRIEL: *Harry.*

[all guests enter the room]

ST. PETER: *Welcome, everyone. Our Father will be here shortly. Help yourself to the jelly donuts and pizza.*

[Gabriel blows some muted fanfare and God enters waving some hurried manual blessings to no one in particular]

GOD: *Be seated, please. Peter, I see here there's just one item on the agenda for today. We're not going to talk about the Jets? I see here "a bad virus". Like a flu, right?*

ST. PETER: *No, sir. Not a flu. Or at least not the regular flu. More along the lines of the 1918 one – only it's called COVID-19. Over a million dead just in the U.S. so far.*

GOD: *Jesus…! I mean – Geez.*

ST. PETER: *It started about three years ago in China where*

13

they ate infected bats, got sick, and it spread around the world. Just about every country has gotten a handle on it. But the United States can't seem to get out of its own way, with continual bickering about vaccines, masks, and testing. And a heap of blame is being attributed to its former President – Donald Trump.

GOD: *The casino guy?*

ST. PETER: *Yeah, that one. Perhaps it might be easier if we took some questions at this time. Albert?*

EINSTEIN: *I hate to keep harping on this but why didn't You do something about that anti-Semite bastard when he first came down that escalator?*

GOD: *You want to talk about what I should have done, Mr. Atom splitter?*

FDR: *Let's talk about what we can do going forward. With nothing but lemons, I made lemonade. Eleanor keeps asking me to write* The Art of the New Deal.

TRUMAN: *How about you write a book on taking a powder when the going gets rough. I'm still answering for that whole bomb thing. Up here I can't get the time of day from the Japanese.*

SARTRE: *Truman, your authenticity emanates from the very existential decision you made in light of the essence from which you navigated your true self.*

HEIDEGGER: *They say I'm incomprehensible!*

GOD: *Enough from you old school thinkers. Let's (hee! hee!) see if we can get Hitchens to lift his head out of that plate of crow and grace us with some of his wisdom, as reconstructed as it is. Christopher?*

HITCHENS: *What? Oh, yes Your exalted Holy Fatherness. By the way, thank You for the legacy admission to Your most Holy of Kingdoms. On this pandemic business. Uh, I think they're going to need a miracle – if that's OK with You.*

GOD: (to Peter) *You've got to love that guy! You have to hand it to him. He stuck to his guns right up to the end. Some of my Son's fan club can take a lesson.*
(to all) *Thank you. I've heard enough.*
(to Peter) *Pencil in a miracle for just before Easter – no sense in putzing around. Now adjourn the meeting. I'm gonna take a nap. Wake me for Hannity.*

ST. PETER: *Meeting adjourned.*

2
Hawking for Beginners

Once again the annual celebration of the passing of Stephen Hawking is upon us. Here is a distillation of the work of this genius down to a more user-friendly form.

Question: *When did the universe begin?*
Hawking talks a lot about time not being real and goes on and on about Einstein's contribution regarding time and space being unified and other stuff about energy and motion and something about jumping up and down in a moving train for some reason.
My answer: The universe started so many billions of years ago that what's the difference how many?

Question: *Does God exist?*
The Master states that the concept of God is not necessary to explain all of existence. Whether this is Hawking indulging in atheistic coyness or an attempt to not alienate the book-buying theists, is not clear.
My answer: Belief in the existence of an all knowing and powerful Creator has become an option rather than a given, that is, until old age – at which point it becomes more compelling not so much as an epiphany but rather as an insurance policy.

Question: *Will robots take over?*

Here Mr. Hawking seems to be non-committal on this issue for fear that a direct answer will scare the bejesus out of us.

My answer: The take-over by robots will be so seamless that we will think that we are still in charge – you know – like how we think now.

Question: *Is time travel possible?*

After a long drawn out discussion of warped space, Euclidean geometry, quantum theory, and something called the Chronology Protection Law – an apparent safeguard against making any changes when traveling to the past – the best I can make of Hawking's answer to the question of whether time travel is possible quite ironically is "not yet".

My answer: Time travel only exists in *The Twilight Zone* episodes. If time travel doesn't exist *yet* but will be possible sometime in the future – let's say in the year 2124, – what happens if some time in 2124 someone travels back in time to our present 2022 when time travel isn't possible yet, how does that time traveler get back to 2124?

What about the questions that Stephen Hawking, lost to us so soon, did not get a chance to address, like:

- Why do old people insist upon rummaging for exact change at the checkout line holding up everyone behind?
- Why do young people at the gym spend an inordinate amount of time at a machine just looking at their iPhones?
- Why do opposing pedestrians on a staircase no longer abide by the stay to your right rule?

What a shame we lost him so soon!

3
The Direction of GPS

The extensive use by motor vehicle operators of a Global Positioning System (GPS) has started to collect critics as well as fans.

We here at the Women's Empowerment Collective (WEC) are particularly concerned with the tone of male appeasement demonstrated in the soft and accommodating female GPS voice.

A driver is directed to make a right at the next intersection. If he fails to make that turn, what happens? A gentle female voice announces that she is *"recalculating"* – implying that his mistake is no big deal – and then provides him an adjustment in the directions, for example, *"make a U-turn as soon as possible."*

Some GPS companies on a daily basis actually receive from smitten men of all ages a number of requests for the identity, marital status, and contact information of the person broadcasting this uber-agreeable navigational geisha audio.

In the interests of adjusting the vocal component of GPS service to be grounded closer to reality, we propose the following options be made available:

Married Male driver/Female navigator
We want to discourage the use of a compliant female voice, a practice reminiscent of the once regrettable popular mail-order bride business. We think that such a voice should be replaced by one with a less accommodating manner. A driver's mistake could

be met with responses ranging from:
Pay attention, you've made a wrong turn.
What part of 'make the next right' wasn't clear?
Are you not listening because a female is talking?
Followed by a directional adjustment with an increasing tone of annoyance with each driver error.

Married Female driver/Male navigator
As part reparation for decades of misogyny, the tone will of course be less judgmental.

Just dating
A missed exit ramp can be met with:
I'll give you more warning next time, but for now, take the next exit and we'll figure out together what to do after that.

Parent guide for teenage drivers
Each missed direction is met with either:
One more mistake and I'm going to turn this car around
OR
At the very first mistake, a Vince Lombardi tone that is tough but character building typified by having each direction stated only once in a "not suffering fools gladly" demeanor with no corrective recalculation and the directive:
Just go home!

All efforts will be made to accommodate as many proclivities as possible. Currently in the design stage is one with a navigational voice coming from the direction of the back seat and punctuated with impatient sighs.

The current all-forgiving female voice will go the way of the flip phone and no longer be the default option. However, at additional cost it will be made optional for a limited time for the hopelessly unevolved.

4
Chewing the Celestial Fat

A recording of a "red phone" call between the Supreme Being and the Prince of Darkness has been intercepted and a transcript of that call follows.

GOD: *Yeah, who's this?*

SATAN: *What do you mean "who's this?" What happened to the omniscient thing?*

GOD: *The Wi-Fi up here is erratic. Satan, is that you? It's been a while.*

SATAN: *I know, but I've been so busy with this COVID-19 thing. I meant to keep it just in China since they've gotten so sure of themselves lately, but since I have a lock on that golf cheat's soul, I couldn't resist giving him a chance to recruit for me. Meanwhile, I scored almost an entire political party – Jesu—oh, sorry, geez – my biggest catch since that Manson gang.*

GOD: *How many in the GOP do you have deals with?*

SATAN: *They're blowing up the phone lines so much down here trying to get in on the ground floor that we have to triage to save time. It's a seller's market. They're not even asking for immortality – just a few more years in office or a job with Fox. I think I have them all except Cheney which surprises me since I thought she was a legacy. On the Democratic side, I'm working on Manchin, but he keeps ducking me.*

GOD: *Adlai and Martin are bugging me to get involved, but you know how I don't like to meddle.*

SATAN: *Tell me about it. I've got Adolph in my ear on how to get Schumer. Listen, let me tell you why I called. That climate thing, is that you?*

GOD: *No, no. I was sure it was you. I have polar bears walking around in circles and fish going belly up like crazy.*

SATAN: *Well, I have recruits saying it's too hot to sin and it's cutting into my Spring draft. I'm sure that puts a dent in your screening process. Can't you work an eighth day and regulate the temperature or something?*

GOD: *Let me see what I can do. I'll put my Son on it, that is if he's finally forgiven me. By the way, that new UFO hullabaloo? That's me. I had to give Albert and Hawking something to do; they were driving me nuts with all the "could you make a rock so big that you couldn't lift it?" nonsense.*

SATAN: *That reminds me, do you have anybody up there that you feel slipped in when you weren't paying attention or maybe got grandfathered in when the old rules were still in effect? I'm asking because I have some real numbers down here that just don't fit in – you know what I mean?*

GOD: *Like who?*

SATAN: *Well, for starters, this Roy Cohn schmuck, what a pain in the ass. And he's still insisting he's straight. Plus, he's got them all thinking he can win them an appeal. And "tricky Dick" ...*

GOD: *McGuire, the basketball guy?*

SATAN: *No, no. Nixon. He thinks that if we let him visit your kingdom he can broker some sort of détente. By now you can probably guess what I'm getting at.*

GOD: *Not a clue.*

SATAN: *An exchange. You know like the U.S. and Russia – a prisoner switch. You must have at least a few pebbles in your sandals you've love to have removed, like say a couple of those insufferably infallible popes.*

GOD: *Nah! They have too much juice up here. Although I am getting fed up with Sheen and O'Conner; we would have to get around the eternity deal we had both agreed to.*
Listen, I have to go. I've got email prayer piling up from this pandemic, but while I consider your idea, I want you to find out something for me: how come they never question why you're always referred to as being male?

5
Unpublished Nazis

Recent archeological searches have uncovered a trove of book proposals heretofore unpursued. Some of the selections currently being considered for publication in far-right circles include:

Oh Fuehrer, My Fuehrer penned by Hermann Goring while awaiting trial at Nuremburg. In this treatment the Nazi big-wig contends that the number of atrocities he prevented Hitler from committing far exceed those that transpired. Were it not for his being a major guard rail against the Fuehrer's more pernicious inclinations, "God knows what would have happened," the bloated veteran addict averred.

Also, while the Nuremburg trial was ramping up, Albert Speer was pitching a tell-all in which he described his boss, the infamous German dictator, as an unhinged ego maniac who needed constant reassurance regarding his meager architectural skills. "He couldn't build a dog house much less an entire city," crowed the "good Nazi". Speer contended that without his constant vigilance, Hitler would have over-lit everything.

Before he decided with his wife to end their lives and those of their six children, Joseph Goebbels tried to get hand-delivered from the bunker a memoir in which he claimed that he was forced to let his wife write all of his many speeches which comprised his years of propaganda for the Third Reich as she had threatened to otherwise leave him for the Fuehrer. He goes on in great detail how she mercilessly taunted him about his club foot, even to the extent of coaching the children into limping around the house mocking his disability.

While hiding out throughout South America, Josef Mengele had a weekly column in the Buenos Aires Gazette in which he claimed that conducting numerous medical experiments on thousands of children was the only way to delay their extermination as long as possible. "People had no idea what crazy plans Adolph Hitler would had put in place had I not discouraged him," the aging fugitive asserted in his account.

Descendants of Eva Braun are in possession of a purported diary of the dictator's paramour in which she describes all the times she distracted Hitler from escalating his antisemitic plans by playing "little Jewish girl" in the bedroom. While there is no forensic proof unequivocally connecting the manuscript to Miss Braun, the family insists that it clears her name of any connection to the worst part of Hitler's legacy.

Just before he swallowed the cyanide pill which ended his life, Heinrich Himmler was negotiating with publishers to release a film of his step-by-step efforts to mitigate the Fuehrer's extermination plans for all Jews. He claimed that he "… was tempted to quit and go public to expose Hitler's final solution plans, but knew that he would just fire me and hire someone more subservient to his ghastly inclinations. Only God and I know how many more lives would have been taken had I left."

6
The Contest

We are happily gathered here at the Mona Bennett Pavilion on lovely Long Island for the northeast regional finals in the National Senior Complaint Competition.

We have collected gripes throughout the area from Baby Boomers to Great Generation folks all the way back to the few remaining survivors of the Great Depression. And while each and every entry was noteworthy, the following five have seen selected for eligibility to advance to the East Coast quarterfinals.

Number 5 – from Stanley Levine, age sixty-seven, from East Orange, N.J. – retired clothing wholesaler

What did these little pishers, like that Manson fella or this new guy with the French name, have that they could get a ragtag bunch of girls to kill for them and then celebrate with an orgy, for God sakes? I'm married to the same woman for forty-one years, happily I would like to add, and I can't get a sandwich without being asked if I'm too crippled to make it myself.

Number 4 – from Patricia Kelly, age seventy-two, from Inwood, N.Y. – semi-retired bartender

Please leave me off the list of people you have to apologize to as your tenth or whatever step in your Alcohol Anonymous recovery thing. If I have to listen to one more old drunk from my life reminding me of how he treated me like dirt forty-three years

ago, something it's taken me nearly that long to jam down into the nether regions of my failing memory, I may just die on the spot. The idea that it is essential for some dirtbag to "make amends" by converting his hazy memory into a thinly disguised plea for absolution simply by having me relive that miserable portion of my past and getting me, all worked up again about what a jerk I was makes me just nuts. For all you other alcohol abusers who have wronged me over the years, either remove my name from your list for contrition targets or just keep drinking.

Number 3 – from Anthony Palmetto, age seventy-nine, from Boston, Mass. – retired teacher

Enough with those ads for the latest prescription medicine to combat constipation, shingles, arthritis, or any one of the myriad geriatric health concerns I can expect to be coming my way during this last lap of existence. Stop airing them unless you can do away with the warnings about all the possible side effects experienced in some cases – like blindness, fainting spells, heart palpitation, severe drop in blood pressure, and in some cases death. Who's taking these drugs knowing about all the downsides? Don't put any more 'cures' on the market until the only downside is hiccups or some yawning.

Number 2 – from Thomas Podowski, age eighty-eight, of Providence, R.I. – retired stream fitter

Why should the rule be that men put the seat back down when leaving the bathroom. How about women have to put the seat back up when they leave?

Number 1 – from Molly Hendrikson, age ninety-seven, of Westbury, Conn

Please have them discontinue announcing who the oldest living person is. If it's a gal, she's usually pictured in a wheelchair wearing an ill-fitting hat with flowers and a stupid grin. If it's a gentleman, his smile looks like it was threatened out of him. No one wants to be the oldest living anything. Stop rubbing it in.

Congratulations again to these five seniors and best of luck in the East Coast quarter finals in Wheeling in the Spring.

7
Longevity

For some time now those in the business of trying to prolong man's expected life span are providing us with an endless list of tasks we must perform to further that goal. Through properly scrutinizing when and how much we eat and exercise, there is no limit, we are told, to how long we can live.

But how is this going to work?

For starters, I'm thinking of the current metrics of Social Security being sustained by the contributions of the employed. So, if I am thirty years old now and it's expected that I will live to the (new) ripe old age of one hundred and thirty, will I have to delay retirement until reach my one hundredth birthday?

And won't medicine have to progress to the point where being stone deaf and drooling are delayed to at least the age of one hundred ten?

And what kind of sleep will I be getting once passed the age of one hundred eleven if I have to get up to pee every thirty-one minutes?

I trust that eventually we'll succeed in delaying other age-related issues like the onset of dementia and political intransigence. Not to mention how piling on all these extra years will have to come with the need to slow down the growth of our ears.

But given how the number of living humans will expand like rabbits or mold, what are we going to do with everybody? I can only hope that one answer is that our current propensity to get smaller and smaller with age will continue over the new longer time on earth so that we will each take up less room. I don't know.

I also worry about an increased percentage of automobiles with turn signals left on for miles.

And we can also expect a saturation of retired movie stars pitching reverse mortgages on television in the middle of the night.

There will also be a larger percentage of the population unwittingly telling the same story over and over. And will the elderly's penchant for proffering unsolicited advice to the young reach epidemic proportions?

What about the institution of marriage having to withstand even a soft goal of wishing grandma congratulations on one hundred years of marriage to the same man. And in those few who accomplish such a double golden anniversary what will each spouse look like after five score years of a growing sprinkling of compromises, spats, and occasional flatulence?

I just think that all these futurists with an insatiable quest for tacking on years and years of consciousness with no end in sight haven't really thought this through. I don't want to seem ungrateful for the efforts of all the well-meaning anti-aging pioneers, but maybe instead of tacking on fifty or a hundred years to the tail end of this finite journey that unites us, how about just adding another decade or two to our twenties? I'm just saying.

8
The "Me-Too" Jitters

My friend Danny recently started expressing all sorts of concerns regarding possible retribution for years of activity with the opposite sex during his several decades of single dating.

I never engaged in activity without the woman's consent – at least implied. I mean back in the day some initial reticence on the woman's part was fashionable lest the man consider her "easy."

Danny posited with a combination of the confidence of a sociologist and just a hint that he was more asking than telling.

I'm no expert on the current "me-too" policy but I'm guessing it depends on how you greeted that initial reticence, I said, trying not to sound preachy. My friend and I are in our 60s, but unlike Danny, I have been married since forever. So my exposure is grossly minimal compared to Danny who, except for a short marriage and two brief "living with" experiments with commitment, has had countless liaisons that could use some vetting.

Well, I never drugged anyone and never made a move on a sleeping woman, he said a little too proudly.

Are you including alcohol in the "never drugged anyone" category? I said now feeling it was time to be preachy.

Are you kidding – no one ever got to first base back then without a little alcohol involved at some point during the evening, Danny now countered – no doubt wondering whose "side" I was on.

Whose side are you on? he exclaimed.

Without answering him, I countered with:

I'm just saying that if you read all the current allegations, they make it pretty clear that included among the transgressions there is a history of male behavior that was condoned by some men and suffered by women that upon careful review does not pass the "consent" test and that a massive reckoning has begun.

I could feel now that my years of envying Danny for his carnal delight-filled years was morphing into the disciplinary stance of a high school principal in charge of discipline for hormonally driven teen age boys.

See? That's my concern. It's the areas of the then acceptable off-white areas now being considered gray with some specs of black, Danny offered as a compromise so as to elicit sympathy.

He was silent for a while and then came his take-away:

Okay, so somewhere in all my encounters there may have been one or two incidents of too many "no's", followed by a booze soaked "yes". So, I have to wait for the allegations to come flying at me?

Amnesty? He blurted out. *Me-too, Amnesty – just like the draft dodgers of the '60s. They also felt they did nothing wrong, but wanted insulation form punishment from those who thought they had erred. Amnesty!* he repeated with what could pass for more conviction. *That's what I need.*

I think you'll have to flee to Canada first to be eligible, was all I could come up with.

I still can't figure out whether his being open to that was good or bad.

9
What? – A Science Primer

From time to time, I have picked up various books that purported to explain, in easy-to-understand terms, some of the most complicated phenomena in the field of science, like Einstein's Theory of Relativity (both general and specific, mind you), the Big Bang Theory and Infinity to name a few.

I've tried to comprehend any "easy to understand" versions of those science wonders, but it has been hopeless.

As I waded through yet another attempt to dumb down Einstein's lauded discovery about how time is an illusion, I couldn't resist noting how long (in time) it was taking me to get through it.

As for the beginning of everything *a la* the Big Bang Theory, my mind would gravitate (don't get me started on gravity) toward wondering what happened just before the Big Bang – clearly violating Einstein's "time" thing as well as not grasping how the Big Bang is supposed to be something before which there was nothing (Is it me?).

At some point I finally realized the futility of my trying to understand these milestones in scientific theory. It could be an extreme overreach on my part in that I am aiming much too high in trying to understand these arcane and complicated fundamentals. Maybe I just do not have the brainpower to absorb such weighty concepts.

A more comfortable reason could simply be that all these

eggheads were, as my grandparents were fond of saying, full of baloney.

Either way, I figured it was better use of my time to wade through primers on much simpler things. And as a result of extensive reading on less complicated matters, instead of not knowing the first thing about Relativity, the Big Bang, Infinity and Gravity, I was now able to not know how radios, the telephone, television, electricity, and toasters work. Perhaps, I surmised, I should stay away from reading about anything having to do with science.

During twelve years of Catholic school education, I had been grilled on grammar and diction by nuns back when, via their approved role *in loco parentis,* they were empowered to augment teaching techniques with semi-mild forms of corporal punishment. I suspect that accounts for my relative comfort around the rules of grammar – though I still argue for the 'legalization' of the split infinitive – the prohibition of which makes as little sense to me as does the theory of relativity – both general and specific.

10
A Generation Skipped

My friend Morty, who is in his seventies, and his youngest granddaughter Trish, who is eleven are very close. Their affection for each other somehow withstands their rarely if ever agreeing on anything. Below are transcripts of iPhone recordings Monty's daughter surreptitiously made of some of the conversations that her father and daughter have had over the last year.

January 19th

MORTY: *What do you mean that Einstein proved that time is not real?*

TISH: *Just that. Time is not real. Einstein proved that time is just an illusion we create to digest how mass and motion within the framework of the speed of light look different from different distances.*

MORTY: *He really said that?*

TISH: *Basically, yes.*

MORTY: *That makes no sense. If there's no such thing as*

time, how would Einstein answer the question: How long did it take to come up with that theory?

TISH: *Ugh!*

January 31st

MORTY: *Bob Dylan was* not *rapping.*

TISH: *Did he squeeze a lot of words into each line?*

MORTY: *Yeah, but...*

TISH: *And weren't those words more often spoken rather than sung?*

MORTY: *Well, in a way but...*

TISH: *Were his works creating a message targeted to your generation about the state of the world?*

MORTY: *Well, of course, but...*

TISH: *He was rapping, grandpa.*

MORTY: *But rapping makes no sense.*

TISH: *Unlike, I suppose, the smooth elision of* Don't follow leaders, watch the parking meters, *huh?*

MORTY: *I'm going to take a nap.*

February 6th

TISH: *Grandpa, who were Steve and Eydie?*

MORTY: *They were a very popular husband and wife singing team back in the '50s and '60s. Why do you ask?*

TISH: *Well, I was showing Grandma some videos of Jay Z and Beyonce and she said that they were the Steve and Edie of my generation. Did they rap?*

MORTY: *Yeah, they wrote most of Bob Dylan's songs.*

TISH: *Smart alec!*

February 4th

TISH: *Is it true that television used to have just only seven channels?*

MORTY: *Yes. And there was no internet, no face time or text messaging, no cell phones, and no personal computers. And T.V. didn't have color – just black and white.*

TISH: *Why no color? If things are in color, why wouldn't they come out in color on T.V.?*

MORTY: *They didn't have the technology yet to show programs in color.*

TISH: *Are you pulling my legs?*

MORTY: *It's* pulling your leg – *just one leg. No, I'm not pulling your leg and brace yourself: there was actually a time when there was no T.V.*

TISH: *I'm telling Mommy you're making up stories.*

11
I.T. Blues

A recent conversation that a Fred and Trudy B. had with their I.T. Support representative was recorded for quality assurance and is presented here.

<u>I.T. Rep:</u> *Good morning, my name is Martin. I'm an I.T. Specialist. Please state your name.*

<u>FRED and TRUDY:</u> (Starting out saying their names simultaneously.)

<u>TRUDY:</u> *Sorry. I'm Trudy and my husband, Fred, is here too. We have you on speaker phone – which our daughter taught us how to do – and we need someone's help with this...*

<u>FRED:</u> (Interrupting) *I'm here too. What's your name?*

<u>TRUDY:</u> *He already said his name – it's Marvin, right Marvin?*

<u>MARTIN:</u> *No, ma'am, it's Martin but that's OK. Let's see what I can help you with today.*

<u>FRED:</u> *OK, let me tell you the problem we're having, Marvin.*

TRUDY: *He said his name is Martin. Martin, let me tell you what...*

FRED: (Interrupting) *How old are you, son? You sound young. Doesn't he sound young, Trudy?*

TRUDY: *It's not important how old... I'm sure you're old enough, Martin. But you should know that Fred and I are senior citizens and a lot of this computer stuff we're not used to. When we were your age... what are you, like twenty? Our youngest grandson is twenty-one. I'll bet you're smart like him; he's in law school so we can't take up his time with our computer problems...*

FRED: *He doesn't care that we have a grandson in law school. Let me tell Marvin what the problem is.*

TRUDY: *It's Martin, not Marvin.*

FRED: *OK! OK! Martin – here's the problem. Trudy has AOL and I have Gmail, and until yesterday we each got our email by clicking on different places on the screen. Now the place where I click no longer works.*

TRUDY: *I can still get my email. I think Fred is clicking wrong, but he won't listen.*

MARTIN: *Trudy... may I call you Trudy?*

TRUDY: *Yes, it's short for "Gertrude", but everyone calls*

me Trudy.

FRED: *He doesn't care what everyone calls you.*

MARTIN: *So, Trudy, please access your email for me right now.*

TRUDY: *OK, give me a second. OK, I just clicked on and it says I have to enter my password T-R...*

MARTIN: (Interrupting) *For security purposes, please don't say your password out loud.*

TRUDY: *Oh, OK.* (She now whispers her password as she enters it.)

MARTIN: *OK, you should see your AOL email. Do you?*

TRUDY: (Excited) *Yes, yes, I do. I see it.*

FRED: *Yeah, but where's my email?*

MARTIN: *Look at the top of the screen. You should see a line of different titles, one of which should be "Gmail". Do you see it?*

FRED: *Yes, I see that, but I don't see any email for me. Just email for Trudy. Where's my email?*

MARTIN: *Click on the word "Gmail".*

FRED: *OK, oooh! Look Trudy, there's my Gmail.*

TRUDY: *Where did my email go? It's not there anymore. Fred – what did you do? Martin, I think Fred pressed the wrong thing.*

MARTIN: *Trudy, at the top above Fred's email, do you see the words "AOL"?*

TRUDY: *No. Oh wait, at the top?*

MARTIN: *Yes, at the top.*

TRUDY: (Excited again) *I see it. I see it.*

MARTIN: *Good. Now click on that.*

FRED: *What happened to my email?*

MARTIN: *It didn't go anywhere. When you want to see your email, you press "Gmail" at the top and when Trudy wants to see her email, she presses "AOL" at the top.*

FRED: *Boy, oh boy, you're really good at this stuff, Marvin.*

TRUDY: *Thank you so much. How do we let your boss know what a great help you were?*

MARTIN: *It's not necessary, but if you want to, you will get an email asking for your opinion on how helpful this session was.*

FRED: *Which one of us gets that email Marvin?*

TRUDY: *His name is Martin, not Marvin.*

After the call ends, Fred tries calling back to find out which one of them should complete the questionnaire. After trudging through all the auto prompts, he is not able to get the operator to locate "Marvin".

12
The Retiring Boomer

Starting in 2011, the first crop of Baby Boomers reached retirement age. And each year since then this group with its incrementally tweaked added life expectancy pile on to this cohort.

These folks born between 1946 and 1964 with their increasingly expanding longevity don't seem to be bothered by being perceived as a financial drain on the still employed populace.

So it is with urgency that we share with you something recently sent to us anonymously here at the *Enough is Enough Intergenerational Office (EIEIO)*. Said document provides a blueprint of proposed legislation that seniors, with their penchant for turning out as voters in big numbers, are coming unnervingly close to getting passed. Here they are:

PROPOSITION: With hearing being one of the first senses to falter with advanced age, lip reading would now be covered by Medicare. (This to be offered to a population that somehow manages to be both hearing challenged and always thinking "the music is too loud.")

PROPOSITION: The right for any senior citizen carrying a valid AARP card, to yank up the pants of any young man wearing his britches fashionably low on the buttocks.

PROPOSITION: It would be a misdemeanor for anyone standing behind a senior citizen in a checkout line to sigh, groan, snicker or otherwise display impatience or disapproval when said senior takes, before paying, whatever time is necessary to excavate from a cluttered purse an applicable coupon to save five cents or the exact change so as not to have to break a dollar bill.

PROPOSITION: Minimum speed limits will no longer be applied to seniors. Everyone will just have to have a little patience. Where are you going – to a fire?

PROPOSITION: Blue will henceforth be considered a natural hair color (applies only to women).

PROPOSITION: While agreeing to be at least respectful of all the changes in the social fabric that they have encountered from their youth to the present, including the use of "Ms.", diverse forms of sexual preference, gay marriage and adoption, and even the syllabus of transgender pronouns, seniors will get a pass on Barbie's boyfriend, Ken, sporting a man-bun.

Hopefully our exposing this plan in its nascent stage will reveal it as yet another gray power overreach by the Spoiled Generation and thereby launch its demise.

On a side note, we're not looking to minimize senior citizen contributions to popular culture, but we would just like to make them aware that contrary to what some of them claim, Jay Z and Beyonce are not the new Steve and Edie and Hip Hop should not be seen as penance for Fabian.

With seniors expected to live significantly longer than their predecessors, we have been hearing the concerns of millennials who are currently anticipating that they will have to reach the age of ninety-three before being eligible for social security. This is exacerbated all the more by science making geometric progress in extending life expectancy such that ninety-three might well soon be considered middle age.

And so, here at EIEIO we are recommending to all Baby Boomers a two-pronged solution to this growing inequity and intergenerational tension:

1) Please drop the six propositions listed above.

2) We'll look the other way if you decide it's time to loosen up and have a little more pasta, sugar, and gluten.

13
Releasing My Inner Scrouge

It was early December of 2021 when my wife and I began planning for our annual Christmas Eve celebration at our home. It was skipped the prior two years dues to COVID-19, so we were especially excited about having twenty of her relatives, of all ages, gathered again for a day and evening of food, fun, and a rousing game of Secret Santa – wherein each person only has to buy one gift but is played with rules reminiscent of Tegwar (see the movie *Bang the Drum Slowly* where a slow-witted rookie baseball player is misled by veteran teammates by ever-changing card game rules).

So, there we were, all excited about Christmas Eve once again. The ongoing COVID-19 protocol in early December was that family gatherings were safe if everyone were vaccinated and boosted.

Then along came Omicron. At first the above recommended strategy was still the rule of the day. Then there were murmurings. This new variant was more contagious than Delta – yesterday's strain *du jour* – and one relative called and expressed concern.

I was on reassurance duty. If we were all vaccinated and boosted (and we all were) then we were safe, I contended with an air of calm assurance.

Until I started tuning in to the daily update where doubts about the aforesaid protocol were being broadcast. Not a 180-

degree turn, but kind of a slow and persistent stream of qualifications usually expressed by the major medical honchos.

It started with:

If you want an extra layer of protection…

Everyone has to assess his/her own sense of risk.

And after several days of this middling-messaging double talk, and just three days before Christmas Eve, two of the experts agreed on the "2 out of 3" rule:

Everyone is vaccinated.

Everyone is wearing a mask.

Everyone has a negative test just before arriving.

Now not everyone in practice subscribes to this "2 out of 3" rule, but I, being situated on the risk averse scale just short of the position held by a chihuahua with OCD, considered this rule absolutely sacrosanct.

We would be maskless while eating of course, but eating is one of the main activities of our Christmas Eve and there was a shortage of at home COVID-19 tests. So, after several conversations with my wife and the more senior of her relatives, it was decided that we had to cancel the party. Well, more like *I* decided and they went along in reluctant deference to my age.

At seventy-six, I would be the oldest person at the festivities, so I wouldn't categorize the other party planners as going along with the cancellation decision as a consensus. I was the proverbial skunk at the party… or more accurately non-party.

It was more like no one wanted to be the one blamed for killing me. And despite my wife's customary graciousness about going along with this fun-kill, I knew this was on me.

These parties consist of just my wife's extended family as I have lost contact with all my relatives through either inertia or death. So, it was clear to all, myself included, that for this entire holiday period, I would have to walk up and down my block wearing a Scrooge sandwich board.

In all the politeness expressed in my presence, any hint of support or resentment was well hidden – the latter of which was dominant to the extent that Omicron was believed to be as benign as predicted.

For my part, I dutifully refrained from thinking about what would have had to happen to transform me from a wet blanket to hero.

This year we had the party and the only people wearing masks were myself and my wife who did so out of nothing but solidarity. And I know that decades from now, some little great grandson or distant cousin will look at the picture we took of the twenty people in attendance and ask:

Why are two people wearing masks?

14
The Other Side

A friend of mine – let's call him Frank – no wait I have a friend named Frank – a friend of mine named Pete was hit by a bicyclist on Madison Avenue in Manhattan recently and was considered dead for approximately one hour and nineteen minutes before being revived. The average dead time, Pete advises, for a revived dead person is just under nine minutes. So, the elapsed time of Pete's visit to the beyond is considered quite lengthy.

About his time on "the other side", Pete attests to the following:

Contrary to death folklore, for Pete there was no white light that the revived dead have traditionally reported seeing when they first pass. Instead, he was given a seat in a large auditorium and made to fill out numerous forms. All paperwork – no white light.

Pete naturally was apprehensive about whether there was a Heaven and a Hell and of course he fretted about which one he was slated for. It turns out that there is neither a Heaven nor a Hell per se. Instead, each dead person is presented with a printout of his life – the number of pages depending on age at death. The dead person is then advised that he will be assigned to an area commensurate with the balance sheet of his life.

The more virtuous the life, the plusher the area of assignment. Pete says that he was given a brochure depicting the area to which he was being directed – something resembling

Astoria before gentrification.

The person to his left, a loud, aggressive male around fifty, was assigned to what looked like a lagoon and the person to Pete's right, a quiet young girl no older than ten or so, was being matched with a place reminiscent of Walt Disney's Fantasy Land from the fifties. All things considered; Pete had no complaints with his lot in li—uh—death.

Before anyone was shipped to his/her new area, each person got to ask any three questions in the one minute allowed. Pete understandably felt the pressure of such a time constraint but managed to ask the following:

Question: *Did Lee Harvey Oswald act alone in assassinating JFK?*
Answer: *Pete was advised that the answer to this question would not be available until Henry Kissinger passes on and is interrogated.*

Question: *Is Einstein's claim true that time is not real?*
Answer: *At this point Einstein was summoned and after given the question proceeded to laugh hysterically.*

Question: *Why are the Beatles the only rock group to whose music you can't dance to except for the cha cha?*
Answer: *It was designed that way so you would sit still and decide whether Paul was the walrus and whether he was dead.*

After the allowed questions Pete was given a laminated card listing some bottom-line perks available to everyone regardless of area of assignment. To the best of Pete's memory that list included:

- *There will no longer be a need for stretching.*
- *One's body will be restored to its age at peak condition (before any surgical enhancement).*
- *Everyone will have the same I.Q. equivalent to our 143. All those whose score on Earth was above that level will be given some time to adjust to their processing everything a little slower and with less smugness than they were accustomed.*

The next thing Pete remembers is someone yelling "clear!" and his waking up with three EMT's smiling at him welcoming him back.

Are we in Astoria? Pete remembers blurting out.

15
Til Death Do Us Part

I got married later than most. I married for the first and last time when I was forty years of age to a woman close to my age. So, I didn't have to tell her who John Garfield was and she didn't have to tell me that age is just a number.

Happily married, I am at the home stretch now as a man of seventy-seven and I can see the finish line. Since this is the only race where the aim is to be last not first, I move at a comfortable canter.

However, being old, married and also retired is a mixed bag of zwieback.

Benefits:
- If you die at home, a spouse will know about it in time to prevent the indignity of neighbors reporting a strange odor emanating from the apartment of the reclusive bachelor you would otherwise be having been dead for three weeks preceded by six days of unbearable agony.
- You may never become completely comfortable with the idea that someday you will no longer be. But since you are no longer used to living alone, you will prefer dying before your partner does so that you won't have to live alone again. I suspect this is not the case for your partner. After taking into account all the years of handling a man's ego and since someone has to go first, wives don't mind that it's not them.

- Once you're retired, every day is Saturday – for most people the only day of the week in which you can both sleep late and look forward to sleeping late the next day. Strangely this is enjoyable even though you are no longer capable of sleeping late.
- Finally, all the people you depend on for an orderly life – doctors, hairdressers, police, and shopkeepers – are younger than you and will therefore be available to the end.
- With all the new time on your hands, you are more comfortable starting up conversations with strangers. As a result, you find that people are nicer than you previously thought – a discovery enjoyed only if you don't notice that you are being indulged out of respect for your advanced age. This newfound need for contact, spurred on no doubt by the realization that you are in the home stretch, is a new outlet for a libido on life support.
- You argue less often – not due to your having reached *satori* but only because you've lost your debate chops.

Drawbacks:
- No matter how many people find you witty, charming, or at least interesting, your spouse serves as a check on how many times you've told the same story when no one else has the heart to. You should acknowledge this as the service it is, but you won't.
- You and your spouse were never meant to have this much shared leisure time so a lot of time will be spent unsuccessfully auditioning different hobbies.
- Just like when you were young, chances are that most people will not think you are all that wise. The only problem is that you had looked forward to one day being sought out as a source of sage advice – but alas…
- You stare! The natural timing that you had when younger

to just glance at an attractive young woman and quickly look away lest you appear lecherous is now gone. You might as well be drooling.

- Patience – gone! The irony here is that you now have more time on your hands to wait in a line but feel that at this age you have no time to waste. Just another paradox to endure.

<u>Odds and Ends</u>

- You will have the new experience of time moving both slow and fast. The days are slow and the years go by fast. Go figure.
- Everything is both hard to hear and too loud at the same time.
- There are three stages to being offered a seat on the bus:
1. You are insulted. You didn't think you looked that old
2. You acknowledge how old you look and are touched by the generosity of strangers
3. You are annoyed that you are not *always* offered a seat

There is no end. And then of course there is.

16
Big Questions

If there is a heaven and if I make the cut, the first thing I will do upon arrival, even before I get the tour, or attend their Orientation, will be to demand the answers to the following questions.

<u>In the Movies</u>
    a. Why does no one ever say "goodbye" at the end of a telephone conversation? Such calls end with either a command of sorts – *Just make sure the money is there on time* – or an expression of resignation.
    b. *All right, I'll see what I can do,* but no *so long,* or *goodbye.*
    c. When one of the main characters in the film needs to hurry to his/her destination, why is there always a parking space right in front of the bank, the courthouse, or the luxury building on Park Avenue?
    d. How does the lead character working in a barely above minimum wage job like waitress or entry level secretary, afford to live in an Upper East Side luxury building in an apartment with a terrace? She's never seen residing in either a tiny studio in a walk-up in Flushing or in a run down two bedrooms with two roommates in the Bronx.
    e. What caused Al Pacino to start yelling in all his movie roles after 1985?

f. Why can't Nicole Kidman find a man not shorter than her?

g. With all the tonsorial talent on movie sets why could they never get James Caan's, Michael Caine's, Brian Keith's, and Gene Hackman's hair right?

h. If James Dean had not died so young, would he have wound up doing dinner theater?

i. <u>On Television</u>
a. Why does rebooting work?

b. Will there be an end to creating new televisions with greater and greater resolution?

c. Did 3D television die because we've lost the exhilaration that comes with youth?

d. Are the possible side effect warnings on commercials for medications proliferating because, instead of full disclosure, we are actually be dared?

e. To be able to skip commercials and to be able to watch all programs when I want to rather than when scheduled, I DVR everything I plan to watch. Did that somehow contribute to my death? Or was is just all the damn worrying about everything?

<u>In Real Life</u>
a. Why does hardly anyone abide by the rule we were taught in school to walk to the right when encountering oncoming pedestrian traffic?

b. In a related matter, why do some people walking in a relatively narrow path in either pairs or even threes, fail to transition temporarily into a single file when approaching an oncoming stroller? (I find that when encountering such inconsiderate groups, to avoid having to step off the walkway and into the dirt patch strewn with dog feces, the best strategy when the offending group approaches stuck in formation is to simply STOP just before collision and one or more of the oncoming parties will invariably fall behind the others and be forced into a single formation.)

c. At what specific age does it apparently become mandatory for a senior citizen to hold up the line at the supermarket by rustling through an overstuffed purse to locate the exact change to the penny?

d. Why exactly is it more annoying on a bus for example to hear someone talking on a cell phone when the same talk with another passenger wouldn't phase you? Some have suggested that only hearing one end of the conversation is what distinguishes why the cell phone caller's voice gets on your nerves. But imagining the call on speaker phone, where you could hear both participants doesn't seem like it would be any less exasperating. Others have suggested that cell phone callers tend to speak louder when on the phone. While this seems more likely an explanation, I've seen people comply with a request to speak lower, and the call still drove me up a wall.

e. When they marry, do lotharios always have daughters due to some cosmic karma adjusting plan?

f. Have we seen the upper limit of how many genders we will have or are there more coming?

g. What are drivers doing 45 miles per hour in the passing lane actually thinking?

<u>In History</u>

a. What is the story with Elton John's new hair? Wig? Plugs? Scalp reduction?

b. Did Lee Harvey Oswald have absolutely no help at all

with the assassination of JFK? Another shooter? U.S. government covert assistance? Mafia help? Or, on the other hand, did he have nothing at all to do with that terrible tragedy?

c. Why did Lincoln and Bork have beards without mustaches?

Now if I don't make the cut and wind up in Hell, I would like to ask all the same questions and then compare the answers with someone who made it through the pearly gates. I haven't yet figured out how to arrange that deal.

Printed in the USA
CPSIA information can be obtained
at www.ICGtesting.com
LVHW021654290224
773039LV00001B/13